Me & My Untied Shoes

B.A. McRae

© 2016 by B.A. McRae

All rights reserved.

ISBN | 9780692699683

"I wanted to see the world differently, so I slept on the other end of the bed."

-B.A. McRae

Infective Introspective

I urge to dance out in the pouring rain and not worry about getting a cold.

I urge to create my own reality and lie myself down in the mold.

I want to fall in love with someone I will fall in love with every morning.

I want to meet someone who is crazy passionate about something.

How I long to paint the life around me and color these people's views.

How I long to wipe the tinted grey lenses they see life through.

The people around me do not fancy my perspective.

The people talk hush amongst themselves about what they are to do about this infective introspective.

They didn't like the way I thought, so they tied a balloon to my wrist and watched as I floated to the sky.

They didn't seem to miss me at all as they went back to their own lives without a single goodbye.

I watched my feet dangle over the world I once knew.

I watched it slowly dissolve into the clouds I floated through, as I then saw other people floating too.

All sorts of different colored balloons, all drifting along to their own beat.

All sorts of smiling faces, all drifting and laughing to one another as they meet.

My balloon was blue as I looked around me.

My balloon didn't match any of the others floating about, until one caught my eye as did the guy who beheld it; like maybe now it wasn't just me, it's we.

He floated over, and like a spark that was waiting to ignite.

He slipped his hand gently in mine, with a smile so bright; with this in sight everything seems to be alright.

Maybe someday we'll float down together and be embraced again by the world that looked away.

Maybe we'll find that the life we left behind was nothing compared to this day.

And perhaps I see the wishes in the sky others fail to see.

And perhaps they don't see them because they were made for me.

If life was simple, I suppose it wouldn't be worth capturing.

If they could see me now, I wonder if they would still ask how or take a bow, for I am blissfully floating.

Reversed Clockwork

"I'm done with all of this!" I screamed, as his blank expression stained my mind, slamming the door and leaving.

Shoving my hands in my pockets and curling my shoulders in, to brace the cold wind, concentrated on the small fog escaping my mouth while breathing.

To be honest I was done, sick of who I'd become, and I needed to get away.

My whole life has been a series of wandering and misleading; I've never really known a place I could just stay.

I was looking down at my feet when some flashing red light caught my eye.

Looking up to discover it was a blinking open sign in the window of a Café, I figured I could stop by.

The small coffee house was dim lit while the sweet slow tone of jazz and piano swept you from reality.

Bad mood or not, when you walked in here, you couldn't help getting carried away with the smooth melody.

There was a modest amount of costumers, taking a seat at a table for two near the corner.

The frazzled waitress smiled and quickly spoke that she would be right with me; smiling in return, when I saw a man sitting by the window I'd never seen before.

He appeared to be a bit older, wearing a grey matted coat and dark jeans, his hair neatly combed, patiently staring out to the city.

He didn't look very well off, but you could tell he wouldn't accept pity.

The waitress came to me, ready to take my order, when she saw where I was looking.

"Ah, yep, he comes here every night, same outfit and all." She explained while sighing.

I jokingly said the coffee must be pretty good then, but she politely smiled and shook her head.

Looking up to her confused, she took the seat across from me and began to narrate the stranger's story, like a book she had many times reread.

"Like clockwork" she said, "More like a clock that's stuck in reverse."

"The same time every night, the same table with the same sight, he sits until close; every day I feel worse."

Gazing over to him in wonder; looking back as if she had discovered my questioning thoughts.

"He comes every night in hopes his wife will too, like they used to, the memory of her passing is lost."

With a shake of her head jotting down my coffee order, I couldn't help but wonder the pain to not remember.

Coming back to set the mug aside my hands, as I began to stand, pushing aside my previous misfortunes of tonight I didn't care about anymore.

I left my lonely table for two.

Approaching the elderly man who deep down knew the feeling of being left on an endless queue.

Setting my coffee down.

He didn't look away from the night lit town.

Pulling out the chair.

Still he didn't seem to care.

With caution I took a seat.

To my surprise our eyes didn't meet.

Contemplating my bold decision, imagining what was so fascinating about his concentrated window view.

With a slow breath he drew, still the window he looked through, his directed whisper grew "You must be lost too."

Along the Oakwood Bridge

Every day we could we'd get our fishing poles and grab the bait from the fridge.

Wouldn't bother putting on shoes, running across the old Oakwood Bridge.

Beyond that was a creek that broke off from the mainstream.

In a way the creek was similar to us, as we sat down, daydreaming or crazy dreams.

Casting out a line, waiting for a bite.

Letting the sun absorb in our skin, the sun was always bright.

Sometimes we'd even roll up our jeans and feel the water run through our toes.

He always knew how to make me smile, as sometimes we'd get soaked up to our elbows.

I knew I wasn't the biggest catch a man could find.

But to him I was the most beautiful thing; of everything else he was blind.

And on days when we couldn't get out before it got dark.

He'd grab some old jars, ready to capture the most delicate spark.

We'd open the jars and swing them through the sky.

Closing them tight, hanging them from the tree, our fireflies.

Casting our lines; standing the poles in the sand.

Lying on our backs; looking up to the fireflies as he slipped his hand in my hand.

Letting time just slip away while we're young, though it's the most precious thing of ours.

Wishing we could stay longer, letting the fireflies go, reminiscing our past hours.

Pulling the line in and walking back jars and all.

Hearing the midnight cricket's call.

For the world was smaller here, walking hand in hand.

Not caring at all that our feet were covered in sand.

Not a care that we'd have to run back to our own houses, right now we were on a ridge.

Smiling to our echoing steps, along the Oakwood Bridge.

My Collection of Stars

I woke up with the hope today that I would see you.

Opening the silky Safire curtains and imagining it in my head as you probably are too.

Throwing on my clothes as I make a quick pose, in the mirror just to check.

Making sure everything looks right, for today must be perfect.

I ran out the door as my feet glided through the autumn leaves.

And if I recall I believe I'll be meeting you by our special tree.

Walking along the paved sidewalk with my hands in my pockets, keeping my pace.

In my back pocket a letter to you, just in case.

I'd imagine you would ask me about my past and no matter what at the end call it ours.

I would tell you my few shining moments, and that I still have a couple stars.

Knowing you, you would smile and say something cheesy.

I just hope today is the day you will see me.

A little ways in the distance I saw our tree, still hanging onto its lovely leaves, placed in the soft misty grass.

My eyes wondered if they'd wander into yours, but not so far as people pass.

I sat under our tree and waited for you.

As it turns out today, this day may be blue.

I waited with my hands in my pockets, wishing you'd come to just even say hello.

Taking a small balloon out of my pocket as I filled it with air, tying the note to you with it, and letting it go.

Watching it fly and hopefully leading to you.

Perhaps today I'll receive a balloon too.

But as of today, I'll be walking back home still with a smile of my face.

Whenever you are ready, I'm in no race.

For it is a shame we didn't get to meet today, but I wish for sunshine wherever you are.

And for it is a disappoint to wait, someday we'll celebrate, waiting for that, I'll be looking at my collection of stars.

Past Dust

I glimpse back at the past.

Feels like its shattered glass.

We all make sins; I say it will be my last.

A promise made to myself.

Put my packaged promises on the shelf.

Life is hard, who'd disagree?

Dust is collecting on the shelf as you may see.

The grains of sand fall from the hourglass.

Watching the time as it pass.

Sitting down and waiting for the door to open.

Wishing I wouldn't have spoken the words I had spoken.

And why do these tears fall when not needed?

Waiting at the door, to you I greeted.

Someday the dust will stop collecting.

And maybe someday I'll stop sinning.

Until then I will be waiting at the door.

Wipe the dust of the past on the floor.

The Artist

I simply ran away.

For simply there wasn't any way that I could possibly stay.

Into my canoe, paddling, slipping away into the night.

I could dissolve into the smoke and unsettled faces in the streets, but I never cared for a dismal sight.

Cutting through the rested water; making it as restless as I.

I just have to get away; perhaps I just need to see a new part of the sky.

But I do love how the city lights melt into the water's ripples.

A compliment to the hanging lights above, like an artist spilled his paint and decided to decorate it with a bright stipple.

No matter how bright the star's light could shine in my eyes.

It couldn't come close to distracting me from your lingering lies.

I couldn't see it then, but oh how I see it now, surely, I must give you a bow.

The layers upon layers you coat on to hide what really comes out before the dawn; it's all just for the crowd.

Advise me this, were your actions improvised, how could you be surprised?

For you wrote the script and played it well, how could I ever tell, this was your applauded disguise.

My part was cut, the curtain closed on me.

For a while I couldn't help myself from peeking around the backstage, just dying to see.

See if anything still reminded you of me and how you could live on.

It didn't take long to see you had already written a new duet and a new voice for your song.

Do I still hope for a reprise?

I'm not one to tell lies.

But life is exhausting when you aren't written a part.

Perhaps someday the artist will make something of this old art.

For now, I'll lie back in my canoe, try to imagine new things the artist drew, forget the life I once knew.

Because it hurts to dream of someone who will never dream of you.

The Tips of My Dreams

Her bare feet hung out the window, and her hair blew freely with the rushing air.

Her smile was mysterious but in no doubt contagious, for she simply didn't care.

She forgot about the world, she left everything but her passion behind.

She discovered quite a while ago that she was lost, and now she wasn't exactly sure what she would find.

She caught a cab and left the only life she knew.

If there was one thing she was hoping for, it was that the fairy tales she used to surround herself with were true.

She didn't have a plan, not even a clue.

Perhaps she had dreams, there were probably a few.

But the thing about strong people is that there comes a point when something snaps.

Everything begins to pile up and slowly breaks you down, and she couldn't allow falling into that trap.

For her small-town heart was meant for her crazy big town dreams.

She acted as if she owned the cab as she still had her feet out the window while in the reflection of her eyes the neon lights beamed.

The cab driver turned his head and smirked at the sight; "So what do you plan to do here in the big city of fame and lights?" He questioned back to her.

She glanced away from her desires, smiled, and returned her eyes back to the scene and answered, "Wait till the tips of my dreams touch this town sir."

The Brighter Side of Rain

I've seen sorrow through the reflection of my eyes.

I've been told true words and lies.

I have seen a beautiful life slip away.

I have had the doubt to pray.

"Why!" I've screamed and silence I've heard.

The painful times of tears without a word.

Remembering I used to smile on any given day.

To now there's days were there's no words to say.

I've been through countless minutes; most I don't remember.

Some minutes wishing things could be the way the past minutes were.

Guilty of loving like I had nothing to lose.

Looking back on the poor dissections I choose.

Trying to go day by day, but it gets hard after a while.

But it's all worth wild, when you make someone smile.

And a long path I have to go, and I will push through the pain.

I dare say I've seen the bright side of rain.

Take Me

Take me somewhere, where I will not be touched by pain.

Take me by the hand, and dance with me in the rain.

Hold me until the sunlight, until I fall into my dreams.

Hold me through all our troubles and run with me through the stream.

Kiss me when I feel lonely, lonely even in a room full of people.

Kiss me while holding my hands and help me feel strong and not so little.

Please tell me that I can do this, please speak with me once more.

Please somehow still be breathing and come through the door.

Run into my arms with your uniform on, on for the last time.

Run to me with a smile on your face and tell me that you are mine.

When I wake, I'll wake next to you, you and the sunlight's gleam.

When I wake please be real this time, and not just a dream.

Pistachio Girl

On summer days like these, there's one place I like to be.

Up in the loft of the old Johnson's barn, with just my thoughts, a cloth bag filled with pistachios, and me.

In my seventeen years of life I've seen and heard it all, that's for sure.

But nothing has taken my breath so many times like the view of the quilted grass pasture.

Places like these you don't see much anymore.

Each morning at six I'd fill up my cloth bag and walk the red dirt path, listening to the blue jays as they soared.

The red specks of dirt would take me to the barn; the only thing I was proud to say was mine.

I'd climb up the ladder to the loft and think while eating my pistachios, and then I'd head back home when night started to hit at nine.

My Grandpa Johnson built this place all by himself when he was seventeen years old.

The only thing he had left before he passed away and told me it was now mine to behold.

For I was the only one to really take in and listen to his incredible stories.

Stories of designing air balloons, meeting Grandma, and traveling the coast; those who passed up these stories had their own worries.

He was the only person in the world I knew who could sit outside all day and smile about the beauty of everything.

He lived a life of no regrets and memories he'd never forget, it is a shame he passed away before the spring.

He told me he had one more lesson to teach, he knew his days were numbered.

On the day we planned to have that talk he slipped away without a word.

That's why everyday I'm in the loft, even if it's rainy and the sky is grim.

I'm up in the loft thinking of what the lesson could be; the barn is the closest thing I have to him.

I know someday I'll have to brush it off and move on.

But for right now this is where my days belong.

So, until I'm too old to climb up that ladder, or the sun doesn't shine.

I'll be up in that old loft, pistachios, and all; six to nine.

As I look out to the pasture, you may think me crazy, or that I don't have much of a personality.

But every time I crack a shell and taste the salty sensation on my lips, I remind myself, there's nowhere else I'd rather be.

Some days my mind gets tired of thinking; so, I imagine Grandpa flying up to Heaven in his favorite air balloon while holding Grandma's hand, as he playfully laughs to me that he gets to get out of this world.

I smile to the open sky, people say my life is passing me by, but hey, I'm a pistachio girl.

The Beautiful Place

The sun's ray's gleamed through the cracks of the shades, as the light reached my closed eyes.

Slowly they open with the memory of nights, the sound asleep cries.

The soft blankets wrapped around me tight, safe in my small cotton cocoon.

Imagining the beautiful day, the blankets will untangle, and I will finally bloom.

Every day I view our precious surroundings we've been so blessed with from above.

Every day I walk with my precious heart; never touched by love.

The sleepless nights I've laid through, the seconds that I've waste.

The ugly thoughts that wondered and leave an awful taste.

The faces my eyes look through and my heart grips onto tight.

Slowly they carve into me, slowly the sun's ray's dissolve into the night.

Lying down in my safe place, as it feels as though I'm sinking.

The bitter taste that bites my tongue, so far away from dreaming.

One ugly thought after another.

As the thoughts chased after each other.

These thoughts always left a word behind.

Words that wrap around my mind.

Said so many times, a pile so heavy.

Gently the blankets tightened around me as it escapes off my lips, envy.

How I feel so exhausted and tired of pain.

How I can imagine you complaining of one day of rain.

How you can choose love but instead you leave.

Finally, I dream of the day I will finally receive.

The beautiful day I will bloom with love showed on my face.

As the blankets hush me goodnight, to the beautiful place.

Your Reflection

The room was still, as I slowly lifted the arm of the record player.

The shiny black vinyl waiting to be played, as everything was left as they were.

Gently setting the needle down, as the room filled with sound, you used to love this song.

Your smile could have been the light of the room; we could have danced all night long.

I remember how I would accidently step on your feet, looking down embarrassed.

As you smiled and lifted my head up, these precious moments I miss.

Each note of the record echoed off each wall.

Echo into echo as they travelled down the halls.

Each word wrapped around my mind, preoccupied with you.

Feeling lost and confused; like breathing was brand new.

It seems the sun sets slower now, turning to see a picture of me and you.

Quietly picking the frame up as the music continued.

Sadness hit my face, for it seemed now to be the only thing I knew.

A tear fell and hit the glass, as the image of you started to dissolve through.

My eyes were fogged up from my tears as I quickly wiped them to see.

Dropping the frame and running picture to picture; you were slipping away from me.

Sprinting to our room, opening the closet, and falling on my knees.

Pulling out our picture box as it seems my world begins to freeze.

Each picture I pulled out your image would fade.

All the pictures of backgrounds on the floor; still the music played.

My body in shock, with not a word spoken.

And if it was just cracked before, now my heart was broken.

Standing with the strength I had left, walking to the bathroom.

Through my eyes my sight seems to be gloomed.

Making way to the sink as I turned on the water, as it poured out at its fast pace.

Cupping my hands under and splashing the cold water on my face.

Slowly lifting my head to see my teary eyes, how I miss your perfection.

As the water rolled down my face and down to my neck, opening my eyes to your reflection.

Surprise

I always loved the thought of you.

How your presence filled my lungs with each anxious breath I drew.

Betting you don't even know the joy to me you bestow.

I was low, so very so; to you I owe, for now I grow.

I grow from you; you are my sun.

My roots are set and done; now my world has finally spun.

But as I've come to notice we aren't spinning in the same beat.

How can I hang on when you've knocked me on my feet; though for now off beat, this love is a treat so sweet and complete, we were always meant to meet.

I have missed you beyond reasons you could ever comprehend.

Your feelings never have to be denied, you've never played pretend.

But the words I've heard you say lace around my ribs and hold me together, until I see you again tomorrow.

Oh, I see, you've put new locks on the windows.

Silly you and silly me, I don't need a key; breaking things is much more fun.

No, no I'm sorry I woke you; the glass is just hard to look through, no, no it's far too late for a run.

I'd love to see your smile this close, why won't you smile to me?

I'm sorry for the shattered glass, alas; this is not how it was supposed to be.

You're screaming, but I'm apologizing; in fact, I should be the one who is upset.

Who was the one who picked up your bags that fell the day you weren't feeling well, now you forget?

Every day, I made sure you were okay.

Oh, now you have nothing to say?

Well isn't life just one big surprise party no one wanted to be invited to, I can tell you're scared, I can see it in your eyes.

You can try to scream, even pretend maybe this is just a dream, but guess what,

Surprise.

Racing the Sky

Looking to the view below and clutching my hands.

Nervous, but prepared to leave where I stand.

Taking the first step; my feet feel heavy.

The thought-out plan; taken in steady.

Step by step, deep breaths in and out.

Every action, every bad thought soon gone, ready to shout.

Taking my feet off the earth, as the wind flies through my loose clothes and hair.

Away the bad thoughts, not a worry or care.

The wonderful feeling as a smile fills my face now's not the time to cry.

Escaping the world, preoccupied with racing the sky.

My Emmylou

Dear Emmylou,

Can you remember when I first looked at you?

I was frozen in my steps as you smiled to me.

A smile came across my face as my mind whispered, destiny.

That was the day I moved right across the street.

How life now had some kind of a purpose, life was finally turning sweet.

Every day I woke and knew I would get to see you.

Rushing out the front door to see my beautiful Emmylou.

Every day we would talk about your problems and things you enjoy.

And every now and then you'd talk about boys.

How you finally found the right one, if only you knew if he liked you too.

Smiling and thinking, if only you knew how much I liked you.

As one boy would come in and break your precious heart.

I would come and patch it up, never wanting us to part.

For I loved how kind and wonderful you are, everyday my love for you grew.

There's just something about you that drives me crazy Emmylou.

For I could never see a girl like the way I see your lovely face.

You may be rushing to find love, but I'll be waiting at the end of the race.

My heart is always yours; I hope someday you see that through this blur.

I hope these words brought out your beautiful smile while reading this letter.

I hope life brings you happiness, and your dreams become complete.

If you ever find you need me, I'm just across the street.

Please always remember to be yourself, for there's no one more perfect than you.

Never would I stop loving you, goodbye for now my Emmylou.

Look with Me

I've come across something quite puzzling that really seems to stump me so.

It circles my mind, all the time, I wonder if you know.

Do you know of other's feelings, their grief, and their sorrow?

Have you ever thought of their thoughts of tomorrow?

This question just gets to me; I wish you could just see.

Still puzzled with these troubles, come take a look with me.

Stumbled upon these troubles, I can't seem to figure out.

Trying to push out problems and wait, but I can't help but doubt.

This feeling that grows throughout me, and I guess seems to show.

With thoughts running around, I'm running on low.

How I wish a human's life could be trouble free.

Needing to take a break from this, come take a look with me.

I had come across something that really stumped me so.

It circled my mind, plenty of the time, perhaps you know.

I've handled grief and sorrow as my thoughts twist of tomorrow.

Twisted around my mind, as my running begins to be slow.

So, all these wonders that stroll through my mind.

These things in life you have yet to find.

The question that puzzles me so.

The ache that grows and rickshaws off its echo.

I wonder if through my eyes, maybe you could see.

See these puzzled things; perhaps you'll agree to disagree, may someday you come look with me.

November

'Hello?'

"Oh my gosh, you're awake, you're awake, I need a nurse in here I can't believe this is so!"

'I can see I'm in a Hospital, but where exactly am I?'

Before I could answer nurses came in and shuffled me out, I won't deny I had doubt, but I knew months ago that couldn't have been our goodbye.

Confused, 'What is this bruise?'

Flash backs of that day, I could barely come to deliver the news.

'A car?'

You were lying in that bed for days on end, I held your hand, but you seemed so far.

'An accident, how could it have happened if I don't remember?'

I cried all through September, barely held October together, now I love November.

'So, all this time I've been asleep?'

I can't wait to run back in the room and begin our new memories and reminisce on the ones that we keep.

' Who brought me here?'

The nurse pointed to me through the glass, as I tried to overhear.

Shaking my head as she left my bed, I don't understand how.

"May I go in now?"

Watching this stranger through the window, who has matching scars.

I'm sorry to inform you, your spouse doesn't remember who you are.

I watched the nurse walk away; my eyes returned to the sad stranger.

Even though the thickness of the glass covered my cry I had to ask why "You don't remember?"

This is the first time I remember crying.

I had always begged for us to switch places; I underestimated the pain of dying.

Their hand was pressed against the glass as the first tear fell from my face, developing my first mental picture.

I loved you through September, held us together through October, now I'm heartbroken in November.

Spoken

The sound echoes through me; this sound echoes through me.

No one will see the things I see.

You never stop when I want you to listen, listen with me.

You will never see the things I see.

I'd like you to stop, stop talking back.

I'd like you to stop, all I see is black.

If you'd open your eyes you'd see.

Stop, listen with me.

Shh, listen carefully, now stop talking.

Hear the knocking?

I'm sorry I frightened you, now we can chat.

I'll just go back and sit where I sat.

I'll just go to bed, but it's hard when you keep talking.

It's hard to go to bed with all the knocking.

Blackness takes over, looking into eyes so deep.

The tosses and turns of restless sleep.

I hate to shout out; you know I'll get upset.

I'd hate to do something I'd regret.

Knocking, do you hear the knocking, perhaps if you stop talking, you'll hear the knocking.

Getting up now I don't want to hear an apology.

You'll never see the things I see.

Running into the room, I see you now, you cannot hide.

You never see the things I see or take my side.

The knocking and talking and seeing, why do you do this to your own self?!

Blackness fades away from my eyes, I'm speaking to myself.

Walter and I

1964 in West Virginia in the midst of the hot and beautiful month of July.

Sitting on a bench at North End Park with a purple Popsicle in my hand, sat Walter and I.

Walter was my very first friend; we had known each other since we were both able to stand.

We both loved seeing the side shows of carnivals when they came into town, eating saltwater taffy, and sometimes we'd even hold hands.

We've known each other so long that we'd still have a good time if we didn't talk.

And most of the time now that's how it was, as I finished my Popsicle and we went for a walk.

Every day of that summer we would get Popsicles from the Italian man with the cart or get lemon poppy seed muffins at Mrs. Autumn's Bakery.

After we got our snacks, we then walked around the town and down the paths of North End Park, just him and me.

But ever since June 24th he insists that I just have a snack, but we still go on our walks, he's been acting very different.

It may be because I'm the only one who talks to him now days, we got strange looks were ever we went.

But we ignored the stares and gossip and enjoyed the summer weather while it was here.

We watched the tall painted face women on stilts as they spun glass plates on a stick and laughed to the kids jumping off the pier.

We saw people falling in love on the Ferris Wheel, and shreds of escaped pink cotton candy float along with the breeze.

The streetlights began to turn on as I turned to Walter and told him I had to leave.

I walked into the house as I was greeted with a cold look from my Mother.

As much as I tried to explain to her, she did not like Walter.

I shut the door behind me and told her about my day.

She closed her eyes and held her hand to her head in frustration, and seemed she had nothing to say.

Waiting for a response she then opened her eyes and began to yell.

As her yelling rang in my ears, I tried to search her eyes to see her love for me, but I could never tell.

"We're always the talk and joke of the town! We've been through this you cannot talk to or see Walter!" she screamed.

"You have made this family so corrupt" she said, distressed, as we walked our separate ways to blow off some steam.

I tried to put what she was saying together as I went to my room and glanced at the large world map stapled to my wall with circled places I want to go, places that are far.

And like something had hit me in the head; forgotten memories flowed in and I knew why Mom was mad, Walter passed away in the car.

June 24th was the day the three of us were going to the beach; it was a perfect day for the sun.

But a car collided with ours and became a hit and run.

Walter was gone, Mom got some broken ribs, and now my memories and reality like to come and go away.

I stared at the map; June 24th was supposed to be a perfect day.

My head didn't seem to hurt much anymore, as I heard a comforting and familiar voice say "Hi".

Turning around I smiled, once again it's just Walter and I.

Strolling Through My Mind

Have you ever decided to take a pause to look back and remember?

As my thoughts look back now, things aren't as simple as they were.

For I remember running across the pavement on my bare feet.

Racing down the street, how things used to be so bittersweet.

How a whole afternoon could be spent at the park with a couple friends.

Making plans to come back right as the day ends.

How consequences didn't come to mind and life was taken for granted.

I used to jump off the swings so high and perfectly I landed.

And somewhere in there I started to grow up.

Floating on in this life and learning lessons to pick up.

I remember seeing Heaven's face in such a perfect girl.

Whispering to myself someday she'd be my precious pearl.

And one afternoon I got to stand a little taller.

The beautiful Fourth of July, sitting by the water.

Sitting next to Marylou right as the fireworks arrived.

Slowly leaning in, becoming the luckiest man alive.

Starting off in the world on my own gathering everything I knew.

And sealed with a gold ring, joined me, Marylou.

Every minute of every hour were memories in the making.

How I wish now I could go back; I wouldn't have missed a thing.

Now, I can't help but feel sorrow remembering by myself.

In a perfect place my Marylou is enjoying herself.

It seems in life we have a fast forward button but not one to rewind.

As I wait now, strolling through my mind.

When the World was Smaller

Remember when an hour felt like a moment?

Or when life was so plain, most things, we had no idea what they meant.

No worries in our world but just to get some extra time to play.

Laughing and living without a care, taken for granted each day.

When life we didn't know had value and we didn't worry about tomorrow.

Looking up to our parents, the adults in our lives, and not understanding sorrow.

When our imagination ran wild and we wanted to always be outside.

Running around, listening to sounds, and building up our pride.

But soon we spend more time indoors and get caught up in life, we forget about those days.

We shake our heads and get back to work and think, it was just a phase.

But some days we think; how if we could just go back.

How we would live out those days and have the imagination we used to have that we now lack.

Go back to when there just wasn't worry, stress, or confusion, when we stood a little taller.

If only we could go back, to when the world was smaller.

Falling Piano Keys

The symphony grew louder in the back of my mind.

As my fingertips gently touch the black and white keys, the sounds of the world were blind.

The rhythm flows through me and escapes into the atmosphere.

Each note so defined, each note so clear.

The beautiful melody played softly at its own pace.

But the symphony was stronger as my heart started to race.

The violins played faster as the cellos followed along.

The piano's keys tried to keep up with the song.

So powerful and mighty the rhapsody played.

Somewhere in the madness the melody had stayed.

The notes came out fast, faster than they had been.

A sudden shock from beneath me, as the tiles under me began to cave in.

The stone crumbled so quickly, as the symphony became amused.

Support failed from beneath me, defeat I refused.

Gripping onto the keys as the base of the piano hit my knees.

My world collapsing around me as it hits my face; the falling piano keys.

The adrenalin that matched the violas pitches so high.

The black and white keys falling on me as I closed my eyes.

Feeling the air hit my back as it begins to sting.

Such a feeling of falling in nothing.

But the symphony began to seem calm the keys no longer hit me.

Softly it was, but I could hear the melody.

Suddenly flashes of light I could see behind my closed eyes.

Like there was string around my wrists they lifted and were set down as they began to untie.

And to my amazement I see.

Lined up perfectly, the white and black keys.

The world lifted back in place, the symphony not a trace, has my world now attained?

Or is it the real question now, have I gone insane?

Thread Decorated in Red

You're so cold to hold, why do I feel a sense of warmth when you're near?

Dear, to make things clear, it's you who always brings me back to here.

Your sharp touch is like a lingering ghost, still as haunting as our first encounter.

Perhaps you should have left me on the counter; then again you always were a downer.

Your quintessence ricochets off my memories; you caressed my skin so carelessly.

Markedly I must agree, why who needs a pharmacy when you have me; I am your addicting therapy.

No, how dare you stumble into my mind!

Might I remind, it is me who's left behind and you who comes back desperately twined.

Smiles are easier to explain than broken frowns.

Sometimes people see an empty swimming pool when really, you're beginning to drown, but it's okay now; just pick me up as you fall down.

Promise me this will be the last time we meet.

It isn't myself who deems to be incomplete, so let's see, excrete me; wouldn't that be bittersweet.

Don't you lie to me, I know how this works and I know how this ends!

A thought you always apprehend, but in the end we're still friends.

Okay then, go ahead.

Look at what you've dread; such a lovely thin line like thread decorated in red.

I can't remember when I had none.

Oh, my Dear you're crazy, certainly, look at what you've done.

How could I have ever seen you as a flicker for help, something as kind as an appraiser?

You saw an eraser; I'm nothing more than a piddling razor.

Echoes of The Past

Honey I can hear you; I'll be there in just a second.

Coming back from the kitchen with what she always recommended.

A small glass of tea which was to be, never too hot or cold.

A glass for each of us, painted with marigolds.

Gently setting them down on the small table, taking a seat next to her.

I had traveled many places, but a seat next to her I'd always prefer.

She was the sunshine of my life, the beautiful colors of my rainbow.

Smiling to my girl, I heard an echo.

But she continued to laugh and chat as my mind wondered what I heard.

As I listened closely now, my Dear wasn't speaking a word.

I turned to her confused as she gently took a glass of tea.

She smiled and took a drink and gestured the other one to me.

I wrapped my hand around the glass taking a drink.

She held the glass with her fragile hands and took a pause to think.

Her lovely smile had slowly disappeared as her hands trembled to hold.

Falling down came, the glass marigolds.

She looked to me with glossy eyes as her arms stretched out to me.

Shocked with what was time for recommended tea.

Tears filled up her eyes as we both knew what was happening.

Looking into her perfect eyes as my hands from hers were slipping.

How sadness fills me up seeing my Dear alone, remembering the time that's passed.

Now we both hear echoes of the past.

Let Us

Let us get lost in the sun and lose track of time.

Lose all the worries on our shoulders, the heavy weight of feeling older, and steal these moments like it's a crime.

Let us hop on a train and never let it cross our minds the urge to turn back to what we left behind.

The soft hum of the engine will drift us to sleep, silent promises we'll keep, as our fingers intertwined.

Let us start a new life.

Though I never thought myself a wife.

Let us make each other's coffee, as we get ready for the day.

All I need is you, somehow someway you needed me too; we'd have a lovely day.

Let us lay in our hammock in the mid-day shade.

While my head rests on your chest, the Earth seemed like but a guest; we were lost beyond the world around us as we swayed.

Let us end our night with a dance about the wrap around deck.

The star's light illuminated our faces, as our feet spun in slow paces, we were the world in each other, though us to the world we were a speck.

Let us get lost in the moon and lose track of time.

Lose all thoughts of reality, because just maybe in this moment they weren't worth a dime.

Doodles of Reality

She wanted to run away.

Funny, because you didn't see her that way.

How her eyes would reflect such a delicate simplicity.

With a refection so fragile how could it cross your mind her eyes are soaked with toxicity.

Dripping with tears from fears that have built up over the years.

But ask her what's wrong and like the first notes of your favorite song her smile appears.

She gave you sunshine in exchange for your rain.

Absorbing her light; too preoccupied with its beauty to notice her pain.

Volumes of jotted notes of rotted faded possibilities.

Reality doodles such a lovely picture, but oh how reality loves to tease.

Over time you begin to notice the crack within her smile.

Though she tries to cover it up, you can see how it can grow to be exhausting after a while.

You struggle to swat away her thoughts that clench inside her soul, oh the things you do not know.

You do not know her deepest throe, and how much she wishes the thoughts would let go.

So, you ask her why, why would she want to run away?

When why indeed would she want to stay?

Forget Me Not

I remember hot days, playing outside day in till day out.

I can remember playing hide and seek, waiting for someone to shout.

"Here I come!" As some would run, but I'd stay in my place.

Stay until I got found but for some reason they'd run away, like it was a race.

So, I'd come out and join in, running into the new game.

But as one strange thing lead into another, things didn't seem the same.

I remember learning the lessons of this life and embracing it all.

I can remember being picked last for kickball.

Going home to tell Mom about my day.

Finding I had nothing to say.

"Just be yourself, they'll come around," She always said.

As the words echoed through me every night before I went to bed.

I remember showing my true colors and taking Mom's advice.

I can remember the days I went through, that weren't always nice.

Trying to make the best of just being me.

Making friends wasn't my specialty.

I didn't see smiles much, at least in a good way.

Now I could tell the difference, the colors I'd tuck away.

I remember being quiet and hardly saying a word.

I can remember the laughs and jokes my Mom had never heard.

Always doing my work and trying to go through till the end of the day.

I'd never say a word, but they always had something to say.

Trying to stay strong, but that seemed to fade.

How well could you cope with always being afraid?

The laughs seemed to get louder as the jokes piled on.

Like it was a game; everyone played along.

I never would have thought I'd be so mistreated.

For I remember when me and you first greeted.

Mom will be okay; I know she's strong.

Soon I'll be okay too; the laughs will soon be gone.

It's sad it had to end this way.

Its sad Mom had to see this day.

It's sad that the laughs and jokes had not been heard, and the pain had never been caught.

Remember this day, forget me not.

Your Painted Soul

How do you know perfectly how to make me smile when your mouth hasn't moved?

Know how to paint a perfect picture for others but your own colors you disapprove.

You think the scars you've imprinted have tinted my view.

The scars you think I'll never look through, when in reality all I see is you.

Maybe it's because of the way you push me away.

Because maybe it's your way of wishing I'd see you want me to stay.

Can't you see I crave your soul?

See you can't feel so innocent when it was my heart you stole.

Tell me you can't see me; that you are afraid of dispel.

You tell me you can't see me in fear of the three words I may one day not be afraid to spell.

The thoughts you say cloud your mind, and you don't want that for me.

Say the thoughts only come to visit you, mind me saying that's something you failed to foresee.

Wouldn't you die to feel something so real?

Dying wouldn't be the particular method I'd choose to heal.

Our strength together has grown; you always believe it's me who pulls us through.

Together our strength has grown me into the person you believe in; all credit goes to you.

You say loving you would be an impossible thing to do.

Say, loving you sounds like my life's beginning cue.

Comforting Inhale, Familiar Exhale

I was doing so well.

Couldn't you tell?

My smile was different; I was actually smiling.

For once life felt exciting; I felt like flying instead of dying, for once I wasn't crying.

I was singing along to lyrics that made you want to dance.

How I would sway and turn to every beat if I was given the chance.

My soul fell into dreams when my body hit the bed.

In the morning now when I arose; no demons twirled about my head.

But like seeing an old photo of yourself, you swore never exist.

All the memories hit you at once; your thoughts begin to shift.

The darkness I had sworn away came back to play.

Latching onto the light I had left; insisting to stay.

I freeze.

Please.

Not today.

The haunting memories replay.

The images, they mock me, they pour out onto my skin for everyone to see.

Everyone can see, no, no it's only me; the image makes me crazy.

The sad thing is the darkness is so familiar; it's comforting in a sense.

My eyes adjust easily as you asked me nervously if I was okay; I seemed tense.

Inhale: I am doing well.

Exhale: can't you tell?

Untouched

Your absent embrace has been replaced by the cold breeze that eases its way from the opened window.

Though at times the sunlight paints the walls I can't help but miss your presence in these empty halls, perhaps the light chases away your shadow.

The window doors have been left untouched since your departure; I have been left your faithful watcher; our memories together will not sever.

I long for the day I see you once more, come through the doors, please give me a moment I can hang onto forever.

Lost in my own wishes, preoccupied by nothing then the details of your face, still you are left without a trace.

I am anchored to your promises of refuge and adventure that we will live out together, or am I fasten to a cloaked delusion on the chase.

Where were you when my solar system was falling down; you knew I couldn't swim yet you watched me drown, and yet still I watch the sky.

I thought you were my stars, a pair filled with stories that were only ours, but you were nothing more than a comet passing by.

Still I remain your keeper perched on the window seat, where I wait for our eyes to meet, hoping you are remembering me somewhere wherever.

I long for the day I see you once more, come through the doors, please give me a moment I can hang onto forever.

My mind has become dusty, my only visitor is passing time, I have long grown out of my prime, a few memories have checked out as well.

Becoming accustomed to the routine days, all blended and hazed, a bad habit of sleeping on the cushions beneath the windowsill.

If only I could remember exactly what it is, I'm looking for, for all I recall is a youthful face with a matching soulful silhouette.

Although I smile at the thought still its reason is lost and cannot be caught, how painful it is to forget.

Whatever it means the cold air will not ever seize, however I will leave it open for you whoever you may be for the day you will stop by, whenever.

I long for the day I see you once more, come through the doors, please give me a moment I can hang onto forever.

Entangled

Painting: something I always knew.

What I didn't quite understand, simply enough, was you.

When the paint brush met my fingertips for the first time, it was love at first touch.

With each stroke I painted, I couldn't explain it, how could I miss you so much?

That smile of yours; familiar with each glance, such a comforting trance.

You never failed to make me spin inside with just a glimpse of your eyes, always searching for a dance.

How could I so deeply miss your presence of all things?

For the only time we met each other's glance is through my paintings.

The image of you always fades into my mind whenever I look to an empty canvas and its untouched potential.

Each time I paint your eyes, hidden within their blue disguise; it amazes me, how could they be so influential?

The kindness within them searched into mine through your thick auburn hair.

Though my close ones didn't approve, my paint brush knew no other way to move, being able to see your face made me not care.

Throughout the years of my life through your wet colors you grew with me.

With me without having to say a single word, I felt like you knew me better than anyone without dripping paint could see.

Because we talked without moving our mouths, and we made memories without sounds.

You even played through my mind when I went off to make my rounds.

Weaving through these sidewalk people like thread tied to a needle, running into a snag.

Crossing paths with another, our thread tangled in each other, picking up their fallen bag.

Can't even leave the house without making a mistake, this is why I stick to paint, holding my head up as I arise.

The reddish locks they moved aside, something pulled me from inside; for our smiles matched and somehow, we both knew why, looking in their blue eyes.

Deafening

Hushed within myself the instrumental softly incurred.

Surrounding me an orchestra; bowing its language, as if I overheard.

I contemplate thoroughly beyond the intoxicating melody,

To open my eyes upon the awaiting, suffocating harmony.

But as my eyelids open and the tone had grown.

The melody had taken a turn, as I learned, I am alone.

Out of my sight, strictly in my mind.

My pupils dilated with the intensity of the rhapsody I couldn't find.

Hastily searching all around, for this must be a mistake.

Astounded by the unfounded sound, I must not be awake.

How the pitch itched inside my ears pushing out my vocal cords a cry.

The refrain drained me to my knees, pleading please; I couldn't defy.

Violins, cellos, bass, piano; they pierce against my temple.

Crammed inside, the pizzicato pried, a classical battle.

The broken off bow strings intertwined the spaces between my brain.

The strings thrust off the piano; penetrate and pulse inside my vines.

My mind being pulled further away from morality,

As the cords separated musicality from reality.

Beating beats against my skull immensely deflecting off each wall.

Welcoming the destructive winsomeness, surely, I will fall.

I will fall into the new sanity I have unconsciously created.

I awaited the shattering clash that dictated, but it seems it faded.

Hushed within myself the instrumental softly incurred.

Surrounding me an orchestra; bowing its language, as if I overheard.

Plagued Stained Souls

He ignored the scars on my hips and held them in his hands.

His tired voice proposed to me for a dance, though we had no band.

Gracefully around the room we spun, gentle in every way.

Though there was no music our movements were timed perfectly to the silent thoughts that escaped off our smiles, that we didn't have the courage to say.

Our steady heart beats pressed together, as our souls melted through.

This life of mine has tossed me about, but for once I had a perfect view.

I was no one's astonishing piece of art, and I was no one's angel for their rescue.

I felt his muscles come to ease, our motions becoming slower as the indiscernible music dissolved through.

Our troubled spirits waltzed together.

When I was cold, he became my sweater, and when he was lonely, I became his shelter.

His lips curled perfectly at the ends; his eyes were nothing less than adoring.

I think I have found the missing part of my soul; someone I will fall in love with every morning.

And even though he can't see, see how remarkable he is to me.

His smile says it all, with his heart beat I don't feel so small, this is all I need to be.

Two wandering souls who happened to find one another in a strange kind of way.

Now turning about in sync with the hushed instrumental, dancing the night away.

The Silo Stairs

Many memories upon memories ago when I was just a small girl.

I used to live on my Dad's farm, who used to be his Dad's; the farm was the only thing I'd seen of the world.

Dad would wake up before the sun poked through the sky.

He wouldn't come back into the house until then the sun would say goodbye.

Mom did all the cooking, cleaning, and sewing; she was always a busy lady.

Even though I didn't get much time to talk to her, I loved her very much, and I wanted to be like her someday.

Then there was me; the only child on the farm and the only one near and far.

But one day while I was playing in the yard, my world paused for a moment when I saw a passing car.

Mom told me that night that there was a family moving into the old house with the broken silo, down the dirt road.

I went to sleep that night thinking about the news my mom had told.

The next day I woke up early and booked it to my favorite tree and climbed up to my favorite branch that had a view of the sunflower field.

Then in my view came a small boy my age, dressed in a slightly stained white tee shirt and rolled up faded jeans, this was a moment I'd keep with me forever; no criminal or bad day could steal.

He came over with a smile and a squint in his eye from the sun while looking up at me.

I motioned him to come up, but he waved his arm and told me he had something even better we could go see.

I swung down from the branch, landing just barely on my feet.

I caught my Mom's eye through the window and waved goodbye as she smiled, then him and I raced down the dirt that was our street.

Out of breath, we reached the spot.

He slowed down his steps as I copied him, then he whispered we had to stay quiet, so we weren't caught.

I nodded and then he grabbed my hand and ran with light feet.

I ran with him, gliding over the tall uncut grass, feeling in each step my heartbeat.

He stopped then I stopped, "Well here it is" he spoke in a proud and breathless sound.

I looked up at the humongous silo, hearing the creaking of the door as we stepped inside, you could tell for years there was no sun light or sound to be found.

The silo was a giant circle that shot up and built on its side was spiraled stairs all around until it reached the top.

He started to run up the stairs, but I yelled for him to stop.

He teasingly laughed at me and told me to come up, because he had to show me something.

And as much as it didn't feel right inside, I ran up with him like it was nothing.

We reached the top of the stairs, where there was a small platform.

We sat down on it, looking down to the ground a few stories from our reach, as we talked about wishes and where we'd like to roam.

I told him sometimes being alone so much makes me want to cry.

He looked out to the crack of the roof where the sun poured in, as he confessed to me that he could fly.

A small chuckle came out of me as he turned and joined me in what I thought was humor.

"I'll show you someday" he smiled and told me off, like he'd show me later.

Every day from there on you could either find us racing through the rock piles of his Father's fields or lying in the soft grass of the sunflowers.

I'd never had a friend until then, and I wouldn't have traded our friendship for a million dollars.

Every day he would tease me that he was going to fly, and he'd tell me I told you so.

And every time he told me we would join in on a laugh, and then let it go.

Then one morning Mom had made us some pink lemonade on one of the hottest days.

We both sat under my tree, peaceful as can be, looking out to the sunflowers slowly turning to the sun's rays.

"You know what kind of weather this is?" He asked me, following it up with a swig of his lemonade.

I shook my head and he leaned over to me and answered, "Flying weather", as I rolled my eyes at his forecast he made.

"There's no weather for that silly, no one can fly" I told him, but he didn't listen to me.

My mom called me in, so I waved goodbye and he smiled while running back to his house, yelling over his shoulder "You'll see!"

That night Mom made the best mashed potatoes and corn; Dad was so happy he began to whistle, and Mom sang.

I took over for Mom as Dad and I keep singing while Mom went to go get the phone after it rang.

She called out for my Dad when we reached the second verse, and he told me to keep singing.

So, I kept on, pretending I could hear the beat, beating.

Dad came in with Mom wrapped around his arms while I kept singing.

Mom held out her hand and we all went out to the car; I could still hear the beat beating.

Dad drove us to my friend's house, and we all went inside.

I was looking for my best friend when I noticed he had other brothers and sisters I didn't know about, maybe they liked to hide.

I kept thinking and softly humming my song like Dad told me, as I looked around.

Everyone was talking in a low tone I didn't pay attention to; it was a sad sound.

I broke out of my song and asked Mom if I could go play.

She shook her head no and told me not today.

Then all at once we all joined some funny looking people outside, I had never seen before.

They were wearing heavy clothes; some of them looked pretty worn.

Everyone was heading towards the silo; I smiled and thought to myself that of course that's where he would be!

I ran past all the strange people around, as someone then grabbed onto me.

I turned around and saw everyone but the strangers crying and wiping their eyes.

And I didn't understand why.

Until we entered the silo, the place where him and I first played.

And down near the steps, my best friend laid.

I looked up to my Mom as the tears rushed down her face and she kneeled down to hold me.

A deep voice was explaining what happened to my friend's parents, even though he didn't see.

"Why, why would he do this, my baby why?!" His Mom screamed as everyone turned to see him, and everyone cried.

I wiggled out of my Mom's embrace and kneeled down next to my friend and touched his freckled face, whispering "I'm sorry I didn't believe you could fly."

Waiting for the Next Dance

Have you ever caught yourself smiling, as others may think you crazy?

Crazy I may have been, for your memory made me smile daily.

The way you smiled when you saw me for the first time of the day.

How there could be no news in the world, but you always had something to say.

Or how stubborn you could be, but you were always there for me.

How out of all people you loved me, apart we could never be.

Whether the day was good or bad or the world had made you mad.

At the end of the day you were mine, the best thing I ever had.

I remember how beautiful you looked the night of the 1960's dance.

The sock hop couldn't have been more alive, if I could just have one more glance.

To see your lovely flower printed dress and curly locks.

Smiling again to myself, sitting down on a bench by the dock.

Smiling to our silly moments, making faces in the window.

As I look out in the distance, Darling, it was so long ago.

I know your beautiful smile is showing somewhere in Heaven's face.

Hang in there with me and save me a place.

How I wish I could have just one more look at my Angel, just a glance.

As the waves crash against the dock, waiting for the next dance.

I'm Home

Each morning when I wake up, the house echoed with old memories.

The earth still spun, the sun still shinned, people still went for runs, people still seemed kind, but my world has stopped, since you went overseas.

Your letters stopped coming a couple weeks ago.

Worrying has preoccupied my time, but my love for you continues to grow.

I try to keep strong like you told me when you kissed me goodbye.

But getting up gets harder, it's become easier to cry.

When I'm lost in my tears I try to think of happy things.

Like the time we attempted to make homemade hot chocolate in the middle of the spring.

Or when I was doing the dishes and you caught me off guard.

You asked me for a dance and lead me to the back yard.

The old record player from the attic was set up as the sweet voice of Frank Sinatra floated in the sky above the lawn.

And even thought the sprinklers interrupted us once, we danced and fell in love again till dawn.

It's been almost a year now since I've seen you; you left just as it started to get warm.

The doorbell suddenly rang; I'd give anything to see your uniform.

I headed toward the door, turned the silver knob, and my hope to see you I'd discard.

Opening the door to find that once again, you caught me off guard.

My eyes lit up as my hands covered my mouth by surprise; you looked so handsome though your hair looked a little shy from a comb.

You smiled and wrapped your arms around me and whispered, "Yes Dear, I'm home."

Behind the Mirror

Every day is like a show you watch when you see me.

Not knowing that this is fake, and who you see is not who I intend to be.

To take off this costume would be a dream come true.

But still I put it on every morning; the show goes on for you.

It isn't very comfortable, but it's worked so far.

You compliment me on what is fake, as I look up to you for whom you are.

You don't wear a costume or hide away your face.

For if you saw me without my cover, you'd see my disgrace.

I look up to the mirror and look at what you see.

Then I take off my costume and see the real me.

In envy of my reflection because all it has to do is mimic me.

But I turn away and think, someday we'll both be free.

This show will end, and the curtains will fall, as my costume falls with it and I soar.

I turn back as my smile escapes my face; it's me behind the mirror.

Trapped in Paradise

Our worlds are very different; our worlds are not the same.

I looked at you through the crowd as you came.

You smiled at my painted face and looked at my surroundings.

I continue to look at you, for we don't see the same things.

You're probably in a rush but still you took the time to come and see.

The happy children with boxes, the colorful lights, and me.

Your eyes turned to mine as you smiled to my joy.

On the inside I am blue, but on the outside a happy boy.

Your hands came towards me as you flipped my world around.

Gently setting me down, as the snow came drifting down.

My smile reflected yours, the moment you'd embrace.

Slowly your eyes drifted somewhere new, how I wish I could leave this place.

And as you walk away, and the snow softly lands around me.

Never will my eyes see as you see.

The snow slowly stops falling, forever I'll keep smiling; our time together was nice.

A smile you will always see, envious I will always be, trapped in paradise.

Past Times

The snow falls at the foot of the door.

While past memories of you soar.

Snowflake by snowflake they fall on the pine and then on the oak.

Trying to get use to not hearing the frog's croak.

Out in the clearing the bears are going to sleep.

Into the grass the deer are starting to meet.

Up in the trees the squirrels watch the last birds take off from their nests.

Up in the clouds they find the rest.

The ducks in the pond swim and make ripples in the water.

The children come around and watch the otters.

Parents are snuggling their little ones.

Loved ones watching Christmas reruns.

Elders are saying how their time went so fast.

Thinking back to when they were young, does the time fly past.

The snow is done falling and the children say goodbye to the otters.

The ducks go to sleep leaving the ripples and waters.

Loved ones go on and say goodnight.

The parents tuck in the little ones they held onto so tight.

Bears are still sleeping, or at least they still try.

The deer are still saying their last goodbyes.

Birds flying south to a warmer home.

The squirrels putting away their pinecones.

The elders turn off their lamps as they think of these rhymes.

They go to sleep, thinking of past times.

Voice

You hear me every day; I'm with you all the time.

You can hear me loud and clear, but to everyone else I am a mime.

I can say things that hurt you, as the crying lasts awhile.

You walk outside your bedroom door and put on your fake smile.

I talk and talk and scream at you, but you don't say a word back.

Trying to block me out, but you I know how to hack.

For a while I'm nice to have, you can always count on me.

Then I'm all you fall back on, now it's not just you it's we.

Now you want to shut me off when you're the one who turned me on?

I know you can hear me still when you put in your headphones and turn up your song.

You can flip the switch up and down, but you know I'm not going away.

Nope, I'm here to stay.

You close your eyes and cry as I whisper in your ear.

So, what's the point, where are you going from here?

Crying some more you wipe your face and say, "You were supposed to make life easier, a better choice!"

You open your eyes and look in the mirror; I am your own voice.

I'll Race You to the Swings

Can you remember when we first smiled at each other?

A spark that caught the eyes of one another.

From that spark on we knew God was up to something.

Now we knew we weren't on this earth for nothing.

You became my sun and I became your sky.

You brushed away my flaws, my loose ends you'd tie.

I'd hold onto you as you held onto me, promising to keep this spark alive.

Reassuring each other we wouldn't have to strive.

We'd go on the swings, tip our heads back, and smile to the sky.

Wind soaring through our loose clothing and hair, never would we have to say goodbye.

Both our clocks were ticking, the sound of ticking harmonized.

Time became our friend, as we were together sundown to sunrise.

Our spark lived within our eyes; we couldn't have been closer.

But now, it seemed the harmonizing was slower.

Your hands trembled to reach mine as I reached out to hold you tight.

Your ticking still echoes through my mind, trying to hold our spark in my sight.

The sky has become dark without my sun.

Captured moments can never replace our spark my Hun.

And as I sit now, I do remember when we first smiled at each other, I remember all these things.

I'll wait for you while you wait for me, someday again I'll race you to the swings.

Not Afraid

Alone I would stand, alone I would feel.

I'd wake up with the sunshine in my eyes, a moment no one could steal.

Words upon words would pile up, the worry that is made.

Everyday sitting in the wait I say, for now, I will not be afraid.

The words come easy to say but acting would take practice.

Taking caution of my actions and passing by the moments I'll miss.

Making my own moments to make up for the ones I've lost and have seemed to fade.

Embracing the world around me it echoes; for now, I will not be afraid.

The hard cover that melted onto my skin is starting to peel away.

The armor is coming off to see the true colors, today must be the day.

All the colors will show, and I may choose to go but the old emotions I'll trade.

For I will seize this day and remember that day; I will not be afraid.

Follow B.A. McRae's journey on

Facebook Instagram Twitter

@b.a.mcrae

www.ingramcontent.com/pod-product-compliance
Lightning Source LLC
Chambersburg PA
CBHW020329010526
44107CB00054B/2042